Believe in yourself!
Dana Lehman

I CAN DO IT

Written by Dana Lehman • Illustrations by Judy Lehman

Lehman
Publishing
ALLENTON, MICHIGAN

Published by Lehman Publishing
15997 Hough Road
Allenton, Michigan 48002
www.lehmanpublishing.com

Edited by Imogene Zimmermann & Tina Hall
Design Layout by Gayle Brohl

Library of Congress Control Number: 2009912358

ISBN-13: 978-0-9792686-9-4
ISBN-10: 0-9792686-9-9

Acknowledgements

I want to thank everyone that has helped me with this book. My mom told us some memorable squirrel stories when I was a child. I don't think she ever dreamed that I would write my own squirrel stories as an adult. Judy spent many hours working on these beautiful illustrations. I have an extremely talented mother-in-law and I am very grateful to have her. Gayle helps me with the layout of my books and my website. I don't know what I would do without her advice and support. Of course, I have to thank my editors, Tina and Imogene; they always help me improve my story.

I also want have to thank my children, Danny and Joey. They give me countless ideas for children's books. Without the support of my husband, Brian, I would have never come this far. I am fortunate to be surrounded by family and friends that think that we can do anything if we believe in ourselves!

Dana Lehman

I would like to thank Dana for having the confidence in me to bring her story characters alive. As an illustrator, each book offers new challenges, just as each day of our lives. May you continue to grow from your life experiences with the encouragement from your family and friends just as I continue to do.

Judy Lehman

It was time for another visit from Sammy's mischievous cousins,
Silly and Sassy. Only one month had passed since their previous visit,
but everyone was anxiously awaiting their arrival.
If their visit to Walnut Grove was anything like their last,
everyone was in store for another adventure.

When Silly and Sassy arrived,
Sammy announced,
"I have something fun in store for everyone."
Sammy's friend Bucky, a beaver, asked,
"What are we going to be doing today,
Sammy?"

Whispe
Will
Mag

Sammy cheerfully replied,
"We are going to be visiting an enchanted forest
called Whispering Willows.
You can do things in this forest
that you never thought were possible!"
Rocky, a raccoon
and another of Sammy's friends, said,
"I have heard it's the most magical forest
in the whole world!"

Whispering
Willows
Magic
Awaits

Bucky wasn't thrilled at first
with the idea of visiting
a magical forest,
but he trusted Sammy.

Sammy always seemed to know what was right for everyone.
Maybe it was because he was special.
After all, how many squirrels have eyes like a raccoon?

On the way to Whispering Willows, they passed Paradise Pond.
A gigantic frog was on a lily pad in the middle of the pond.
Bucky saw it right away. Sammy knew that Bucky loved frogs and said,
"Why don't you swim out there and get that frog, Bucky?
You can bring him with us to Whispering Willows."

Sammy yelled back, "We are going to build a tree house."
Everyone was excited… except Silly.
Silly sadly replied, "I can't build a tree house. I always hurt myself!"
Bucky shouted back, "Remember that you can do anything
if you believe in yourself!"

Sammy could see the tree that he had already selected for their tree house.
He let go of the last branch and landed in front
of one of the most magnificent trees any of them had ever seen.

Sassy was the last to approach
the tree. But instead of grabbing
a branch, Sassy grabbed a snake!
She and the snake slid
and fell to the ground.
Rocky ran over to help.
"Are you okay, Sassy?"
"Yeah, I didn't realize
that was a snake!" Sassy replied.

"Welcome to Whispering Willows!"
announced Willy, the tree.
All of Sammy's friends gasped.
Bucky said, "I never saw a talking tree before!"
Sammy replied, "You will see a lot of things here
that you have never seen before."

"Are you ready to start building your tree house?" Willy asked.
"We don't have any tools. How can we build a tree house?" asked Silly.
Supplies began magically falling from tree limbs as Willy said,
"This is a magical forest. I am providing you with everything
you will need to build your tree house."
Everyone was eager to start…except Silly.

Bucky grabbed some wood
and started climbing the tree.
Silly stood there looking up
at this beautiful, magnificent tree,
thinking, "Can I really build
a tree house without hurting myself?"

Bucky could see Silly's hesitation
and yelled, "Come on up, Silly!
I'll help you!"

Bucky gave Silly a hammer and nails, and they started building their tree house.
They constructed the log floor very quickly. Not long after,
Silly smashed his paw. He threw down the hammer and yelled,
"I told you I can't build things! I always hurt myself!"

Sassy looked up at Silly and was astonished at what she saw!
Silly's eyes alone seemed to be floating in midair!
Everyone was shocked!

Willy said, "Everyone please calm down!
Silly turned invisible because
he doesn't have the confidence
to believe in himself.
Remember that you are in a magical forest.
You can do anything
if you believe in yourself."

Rocky asked, "Can you make him appear
to us again?" Willy said, "No… I'm afraid
that he's the only one that can do that."
Sammy asked, "How?" Willy replied,
"When he believes that he can overcome his fear
of getting hurt, he will appear to you again.
Until then…he will remain invisible."

Sammy thought that the best thing to do was to continue building their tree house. Maybe that would keep everyone's mind off of Silly's disappearing.

Once they had the floor and the walls done, they proceeded to start working on the roof.

Bucky went up to Silly and handed him Whopper.
Silly asked, "Why are you giving me Whopper?" Bucky said, "He's good luck!"
Then he continued pounding nails in the roof.

Sammy was watching Silly and Bucky.
Sammy was touched that Bucky would give Silly
a frog that he clearly loved, and so was Silly.
Silly realized that with lots of practice and confidence, Bucky
had been able to swim out to get Whopper in Paradise Pond.
It made him think that with practice and confidence,
he could build this tree house, too.

Silly turned to Bucky and asked, "May I have that hammer?"
Bucky gladly handed him the hammer.
They all continued working, and slowly Silly appeared again.
Everyone smiled in delight.

When the tree house was finished, Silly looked at his friends and said,
"I believed I could do it, and I did it!"
Sammy replied, "Yeah…it's like magic isn't it?"

Why didn't Silly want Bucky to go get that frog in Paradise Pond?

What did Sammy know about Bucky's swimming abilities that Silly didn't know?

Do you think Sammy's words of encouragement helped Bucky?

What are some things you encourage your friends to do?

Have you ever built a tree house?

Should Silly have given up just because he hurt himself?

Why did Bucky give Silly his frog?

How do you get better at doing or building things?

Do you believe that with practice and confidence
you can do anything if you believe in yourself?

Just for fun
Each page has a hidden frog or snake in the illustrations.
Can you find the frogs and snakes hidden in each illustration?

A Word from the Author

As you may have already guessed, I think that you can do anything if you believe in yourself. You have to be confident, persistent, and determined to achieve your dreams.

An essential part of being successful in life is having good self-esteem. Have you ever tried to do something but kept thinking, "I can't do this?" How many times have you successfully accomplished something with that frame of mind? On the other hand, how often did you attack something with a Can-Do attitude? You were determined not to fail and didn't take no for an answer. Chances are that you were successful and accomplished your goal. What you think about yourself plays a huge role in your success.

I was fortunate to have had a lot of encouragement from my family and friends. I want to take this opportunity to encourage you to follow your dreams and always have the attitude that **YOU CAN DO IT!** I followed my dreams, so you are now reading my third children's book. Whatever your dreams may be, they are never unattainable. If you think your dreams might be too big, still move forward and take one step at a time…

They did it!

I Can Do It! is Dana and Judy's third boo[k]
in the Walnut Grove Series.
They work together to bring these tales
of Sammy and his friends to children.
All books in this series
deal with character development.
The first book,
*Adventures at Walnut Grove:
A Lesson about Teasing,*
teaches children to treat others
as they would like to be treated.
The second book in this series,
I DOUBLE Dare You!,
is about taking responsibility
for your own actions and peer pressure.

Dana resides in Allenton, Michigan with her husband and their two children.
Her children and love of nature continually inspire her to keep writing children's books.

Dana's mother-in-law, Judy Lehman, is her illustrator.
Judy Lehman has been an artist and teacher for thirty-eight years. Judy's passion is watercolors.
She currently resides in Hubbard Lake, Michigan with her husband.